real baby animals

billy and bonnie the goats

by Gisela Buck and Siegfried Buck

For a free color catalog describing Gareth Stevens Publishing's list of high-quality books and multimedia programs, call 1-800-542-2595 (USA) or 1-800-461-9120 (Canada). Gareth Stevens Publishing's Fax: (414) 225-0377. See our catalog, too, on the World Wide Web: http://gsinc.com

Library of Congress Cataloging-in-Publication Data available upon request from publisher. Fax: (414) 225-0377 for the attention of the Publishing Records Department.

ISBN 0-8368-1508-4

First published in North America in 1997 by
Gareth Stevens Publishing
1555 North RiverCenter Drive, Suite 201
Milwaukee, Wisconsin 53212 USA

This edition first published in 1997 by Gareth Stevens, Inc. Original edition © 1994 by Kinderbuchverlag KBV Luzern, Sauerländer AG, Aarau, Switzerland, under the title *Flori und Florine, die beiden Ziegen*. Translated from the German by John E. Hayes. Adapted by Gareth Stevens, Inc. All additional material supplied for this edition © 1997 by Gareth Stevens, Inc.

Photographer: Elvig Hansen
Watercolor artist: Wolfgang Kill
Series editors: Barbara J. Behm and Patricia Lantier-Sampon
Editorial assistants: Diane Laska, Jamie Daniel, and Rita Reitci

All rights to this edition reserved to Gareth Stevens, Inc. No part of this book may be reproduced, stored in a retrieval system, or transmitted in any form, or by any means, electronic, mechanical, photocopying, recording, or otherwise without the prior written permission of the publisher except for the inclusion of brief quotations in an acknowledged review.

Printed in Mexico

1 2 3 4 5 6 7 8 9 01 00 99 98 97

Gareth Stevens Publishing
MILWAUKEE

If you visit a farm, you might meet a goat.

This female, called a doe or nanny, will soon have babies called kids.

She gives birth to two kids named Billy and Bonnie. Billy is a billy goat, or male goat. Bonnie is a doe, or female goat. The mother licks the kids dry.

Billy and Bonnie stand up right away.

They are ready to explore their home.

The kids are hungry. They drink milk, or nurse, from their mother's body.

The kids and their mother sniff one another. For the rest of their lives, they will know each other by this scent, or smell.

The sound goats make is called a "bleat."

Mother and baby bleat softly to each other.

What does the goat from the next stall want?
The mother goat lowers her head to frighten
the goat. Billy tries to get a look.

Billy and Bonnie's mother does
not let the visitor into the stall.
She pushes the goat away.

Billy and Bonnie peek into the next stall. They see the neighbor goat has two kids, too!

The four kids look at one another.
They want to play together.

The temptation is too great.

Time for some fun!

Billy and Bonnie hop quickly to join the other goats. They head outside to play.

Bonnie is a little cautious.

But Billy jumps straight into the air!

The kids race each other.

Come on, follow them!

The kids go on an adventure.

Where do these stairs lead?

Goats are good jumpers. Billy does the broad jump.

Bonnie likes the high jump.

All the fun makes Billy and Bonnie hungry again. They drink some milk from their mother's body.

Billy and Bonnie know exactly what to do to get their tummies full of their mother's milk.

Baby goats eat plants, too.

They enjoy a nice tulip or two.

The kids nuzzle one of the farm cats.

But another one of the cats keeps its distance.

Billy and Bonnie are now two months old. Their horns are beginning to grow.

At four months old, they will join a herd of goats.

Further Reading and Videos

Animal Families (series). (Gareth Stevens)
Barnyard Babies. (Video 11)
Caper the Kid. Jane Burton (Gareth Stevens)
Farm Animals. Animals at a Glance (series). Isabella Dudek (Gareth Stevens)
Farm Babies and Their Mothers. (Phoenix/BFA)
The Gruff Brothers. William H. Hooks (Gareth Stevens)
Mammals and Their Young. (National Geographic)
Mother Nature: When Goats Go Climbing. (Discovery Channel)
Seven Hundred Kids on Grampa's Farm. Morris (Dutton)
Wildlife Identification: Sheep and Goats. (Creative Educational)
Woolly Sheep and Hungry Goats. Fowler (Childrens Press)

Fun Facts about Goats

Did you know . . .

— goats often have a "beard" of long hair on their chins?
— domestic goats can be found everywhere in the world except the Arctic and the Antarctic?
— nanny goats almost always give birth to twins, but sometimes they have triplets (three kids) or quadruplets (four kids)?
— Angora goats have long, silky hair that is used for making mohair yarn? (The yarn is then used to make clothing.)
— goats are known for being able to eat just about anything?

Glossary-Index

adventure — an exciting or remarkable experience; a new activity where the outcome is unknown (p. 16).

billy goat — a popular name for a male goat. The proper term for a male goat is *buck* (p. 3).

bleat — to make a rapid "mah-ah-ah" cry. Goats, sheep, and calves all bleat (p. 7).

cautious — careful (p. 14).

explore — to look around in order to discover what is there (p. 4).

herd — a number of similar animals that live together (p. 22).

kids — young goats under one year of age (pp. 2, 3, 5, 6, 10, 11, 15, 16, 21).

nanny goat — a popular name for a female goat. The proper term for a female goat is *doe* (pp. 2, 3).

neighbor — someone living near or right next door to another (p. 10).

nurse — when a mammal baby drinks milk from its mother's breast for nourishment (p. 5).

nuzzle — to rub or touch with the nose (p. 21).

scent — a specific and particular smell (p. 6).

stall — a compartment for a domestic animal in a stable or a barn (pp. 8, 9, 10).

temptation — anything that strongly invites one to do something (p. 12).